Sheep Trick or Treat

Nancy Shaw

Sheep Trick or Treat

illustrated by Margot Apple

Houghton Mifflin Company   Boston 1997

For Margot
— N.S.

For Jack Werner and Pixie Lauer
and all the kids at the Harbor Children's Center
— M.A.

Text copyright © 1997 by Nancy Shaw
Illustrations copyright © 1997 by Margot Apple

For information about this and other Houghton Mifflin
trade and reference books and multimedia products,
visit The Bookstore at Houghton Mifflin on the World
Wide Web at http://www.hmco.com/trade/.

The text of this book is set in 24 point Garamond 3.
The illustrations colored pencil, reproduced in full color.

Library of Congress Cataloging-in-Publication Data

Shaw, Nancy (Nancy E.)
  Sheep trick or treat / by Nancy Shaw ; illustrated by Margot
Apple.
  p. cm.
  Summary: When sheep dress up to go trick-or-treating
at a nearby farm, their costumes scare away some wolves
lurking in the woods.
  ISBN 0-395-84168-2
  [1. Halloween — Fiction. 2. Sheep — Fiction.
3. Domestic animals — Fiction. 4. Stories in rhyme.]
I. Apple, Margot, ill. II. Title.
PZ8.3.S5334Sj 1997   96-43140
[E]dc20   CIP
                    AC

Manufactured in the United States of America

WOZ 10 9 8 7 6 5 4 3 2 1

As the Halloween moon rises,

Sheep are fixing up disguises.

They make a mask with glue and tape

And a monster suit with a shiny cape.

Sheep snip and sew and drape

A costume for a giant ape.

Sheep shape wool in pointy clumps
To make a dinosaur with bumps.

Sheep rip scraps for mummy wraps.

Sheep pose in spooky clothes.

Sheep take lanterns. Arm in arm,

They set off for a nearby farm.

The Dell

In the woods, they give three cheers.

A sleepy wolf perks up his ears.

Sheep amble to the dell.

They reach the barn and ring the bell.

Sheep bleat. Trick or treat!

Animals give them things to eat.

The horses' treats go in with thumps:

Apples, oats, and sugar lumps.

Spiders give a dried-up fly.

Sheep decide to pass it by.

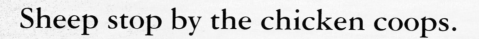
Sheep stop by the chicken coops.

Chickens give them fresh eggs. Oops!

Cows offer hay and clover.

Now the trick-or-treating's over.

Back through the woods the sheep parade.

It's dark, but they are not afraid.

Rustling noises come from trees.

Is someone there, or just a breeze?

Wolves peek out from hiding places.

The Dell

Wolves see scary lit-up faces.

Wolves skedaddle.

Sheep skip past.

They settle down with treats at last.